# MRS PEPPERPOT

## *to the Rescue*

### and other stories

Also available

*Little Old Mrs Pepperpot*
*Mrs Pepperpot Again*
*Mrs Pepperpot's Year*
*Mrs Pepperpot's Outing*
*Mrs Pepperpot in the Magic Wood*
*Mrs Pepperpot Stories*

# MRS PEPPERPOT

## *to the Rescue*

### and other stories by

ALF PRØYSEN

*Translated by Marianne Helweg*
*Illustrated by Björn Berg*

**RED FOX**

MRS PEPPERPOT TO THE RESCUE
A RED FOX BOOK 978 1 849 41802 7
First published in Great Britain by Hutchinson in 1963

This edition published 2012

1 3 5 7 9 10 8 6 4 2

Copyright © Alf Prøysen, 1960
English translation © Hutchinson 1963

The Random House Group Limited supports the Forest Stewardship Council (FSC®),
the leading international forest certification organization. Our books carrying the FSC
label are printed on FSC®-certified paper. FSC is the only forest certification scheme
endorsed by the leading environmental organizations, including Greenpeace. Our
paper procurement policy can be found at www.randomhouse.co.uk/environment.

MIX
Paper from
responsible sources
FSC® C016897

Set in Bembo 13/15

Red Fox Books are published by Random House Children's Publishers UK,
61–63 Uxbridge Road, London W5 5SA

www.randomhousechildrens.co.uk
www.totallyrandombooks.co.uk
www.randomhouse.co.uk

Addresses for companies within The Random House Group Limited can be found at:
www.randomhouse.co.uk/offices.htm

THE RANDOM HOUSE GROUP Limited Reg. No. 954009

A CIP catalogue record for this book is available from the British Library.

Printed and bound in Great Britain by CPI Bookmarque, Croydon, CR0 4TD

# Contents

# MRS PEPPERPOT
## *to the Rescue*
### and other stories

# Mrs Pepperpot to the Rescue

When it is breaking-up day at the village school, and the summer holidays are about to begin, all the children bring flowers to decorate the school. They pick them in their own gardens or they get them from their uncles and aunts, and then they carry their big bunches along the road, while they sing and shout because it is the end of term. Their mother and fathers wave to them from the windows and wish them a happy breaking-up day.

But in one window stands a little old woman who just watches the children go by. That is Mrs Pepperpot.

She has no one now to wish a happy breaking-up day, for all her own children are long since grown up and gone away, and none of the young ones think of asking her for flowers.

At least, that's not quite true; I do know of one little girl who picked flowers in Mrs Pepperpot's garden. But that was several years

1

ago, not long after the little old woman first started shrinking to the size of a pepperpot at the most inconvenient moments.

That particular summer Mrs Pepperpot's garden was fairly bursting with flowers: there were white lilac with boughs almost laden to the ground, blue and red anemones on strong, straight stalks, poppies with graceful nodding yellow heads and many other lovely flowers. But no one had asked Mrs Pepperpot for any of them, so she just stood in her window and watched as the children went by, singing and shouting, on their way to the breaking-up day at school.

The very last to cross the yard in front of her house was a little girl, and she was walking, oh, so slowly, and carried nothing in her hands. Mrs Pepperpot's cat was lying on the doorstep and greeted her with a 'Miaow!' But the little girl only made a face and said, 'Stupid animal!' And when Mrs Pepperpot's dog, which was chained to the wall, started barking and wagging his tail the little girl snapped, 'Hold your tongue!'

Then Mrs Pepperpot opened the window to throw a bone out to the dog and the little girl whirled round and shouted angrily, 'Don't you throw that dirty bone on my dress!'

That was enough. Mrs Pepperpot put her hands on her hips and told the little girl that no one had any right to cross the yard in front of her house and throw insulting words at her or her cat and dog, which were doing no harm to anybody.

The little girl began to cry. 'I want to go home,' she sobbed. 'I've an awful pain in my tummy and I don't want to go to the breaking-up party! Why should I go when I have a pain in my tummy?'

'Where's your mother, child?' asked Mrs Pepperpot.

'None of your business!' snapped the girl.

'Well, where's your father, then?' asked Mrs Pepperpot.

'Never you mind!' said the girl, still more rudely. 'But if you want to know why I don't want to go to school today it's because I haven't any flowers. We haven't a garden, anyway, as we've only been here since Christmas. But Dad's going to build us a house now that he's working at the ironworks, and then we'll have a garden. My mum makes paper flowers and does the paper round, see? Anything more you'd like to know? Oh well, I might as well go to school, I suppose. Teacher can say what she likes – I don't care! If *she'd* been going from school to school for three years she wouldn't know much either! So blow her and her flowers!' And the little girl stared defiantly at Mrs Pepperpot.

Mrs Pepperpot stared back at the little girl and then she said: 'That's the spirit! But I think I can help you with the flowers. Just you go out in the garden and pick some lilac and anemones and poppies and anything else you like. I'll go and find some paper for you to wrap them in.'

So the girl went into the garden and started picking flowers while Mrs Pepperpot went indoors for some paper. But just as she was coming back to the door she shrank!

Roly Poly! And there she was, tucked up in the paper like jam in a pudding, when the little girl came running back with her arms full of flowers.

'Here we are!' shouted the little girl.

'And here *we* are!' said Mrs Pepperpot as she disentangled herself from the paper. 'Don't be scared; this is something that happens to me from time to time, and I never know when I'm

going to shrink. But now I've got an idea; I want you to pop me in your satchel and take me along with you to school. We're going to have a game with them all! What's your name, by the way?'

'It's Rita,' said the little girl who was staring at Mrs Pepperpot with open mouth.

'Well, Rita, don't just stand there. Hurry up and put the paper round those flowers. There's no time to lose!'

When they got to the school the breaking-up party was well under way, and the teacher didn't look particularly pleased even when Rita handed her the lovely bunch of flowers. She just nodded and said, 'Thanks.'

'Take no notice,' said Mrs Pepperpot from Rita's satchel.

'Go to your desk,' said the teacher. Rita sat down with her satchel on her knee.

'We'll start with a little arithmetic,' said the teacher. 'What are seven times seven?'

'Forty-nine!' whispered Mrs Pepperpot from the satchel.

'Forty-nine!' said Rita.

This made the whole class turn and stare at Rita, for up to now she had hardly been able to count to thirty! But Rita stared back at them and smiled. Then she stole a quick look at her satchel.

'What's that on your lap?' asked the teacher. 'Nobody is allowed to use a crib. Give me your satchel at once!'

So Rita had to carry it up to the teacher's desk where it was hung on a peg.

The teacher went on to the next question: 'If we take fifteen from eighteen what do we get?'

All the children started counting on their fingers, but Rita saw that Mrs Pepperpot was sticking both her arms and one leg out of the satchel.

'Three!' said Rita before the others had had time to answer.

This time nobody suspected her of cheating and Rita beamed all over while Mrs Pepperpot waved to her from between the pages of her exercise book.

The teacher was quite amazed at this answer, but she had to admit that Rita was right. Then she made an announcement.

'Children,' she said, 'I have decided to award a treat to the one of you who gave the most right answers. Rita gave me all the right answers, so she is the winner, and she will be allowed to serve coffee to the teachers in the staff-room afterwards.'

Rita felt very pleased and proud; she was so used to getting meals ready when she was alone at home that she was sure she could manage this all right. So, when the other children went home, she took her satchel from the teacher's desk and went out into the kitchen. But, oh dear, it wasn't a bit like home! The coffee-pot was far too big and the huge cake with icing on it was very different from the plate of bread-and-dripping she usually got ready for her parents at home. Luckily the cups and saucers and plates and spoons had all been laid out on the table beforehand. All the same, it seemed too much to Rita, and she just sat down and cried. In a moment she heard the sound of scratching from the satchel, and out stepped Mrs Pepperpot.

'If you're the girl I take you for,' said the little old woman, putting her hands on her hips, 'you won't give up half-way like this! Come on, just you lift me up on the table, we'll soon have this job done. As far as I could see from my hiding place, there are nine visiting teachers and your own Miss Snooty. That makes two cups of water and two dessertspoons of coffee per person – which makes twenty cups of water and twenty dessertspoons of coffee in all – right?'

'I think so. Oh, you're wonderful!' said Rita, drying her tears. 'I'll measure out the water and coffee at once, but I don't know how I'm going to cut up that cake!'

'That'll be all right,' said Mrs Pepperpot. 'As

far as I can see the cake is about ninety paces
– my paces – round. So if we divide it by ten
that'll make each piece nine paces. But that
will be too big for each slice, so we'll divide
nine by three and make each piece three paces
thick. Right?'

'I expect so,' said Rita, who was getting a bit
lost.

'But first we must mark a circle in the middle
of the cake,' went on Mrs Pepperpot. 'Lift me
up on your hand, please.'

Rita lifted her carefully on to her hand.

'Now take me by the legs and turn me
upside down. Then, while you swing me round,
I can mark a circle with one finger in the icing.
Right; let's go!'

So Rita swung Mrs Pepperpot round upside
down and the result was a perfect little circle
drawn right in the middle of the cake.'

'Crumbs are better than no bread!' said Mrs
Pepperpot as she stood there, swaying giddily
and licking her finger. 'Now I'll walk right
round the cake, and at every third step I want
you to make a little notch in the icing with the
knife. Here we go!

'One, two, three, notch!'

One, two, three, notch!
One, two, three, notch!'

And in this way Mrs Pepperpot marched all round the cake, and Rita notched it so that it made exactly thirty slices when it was cut.

When they had finished someone called from the staff-room: 'Where's that clever girl with the coffee? Hurry up and bring it in, dear, then you can fetch the cake afterwards.'

Rita snatched up the big coffee-pot, which was boiling now, and hurried in with it, and Mrs Pepperpot stood listening to the way the teachers praised Rita as she poured the coffee into the cups with a steady hand.

After a while she came out for the cake. Mrs Pepperpot clapped her hands: 'Well done, Rita! There's nothing to worry about now.'

But she shouldn't have said that, for while she was listening to the teachers telling Rita again how clever she was, she suddenly heard that Miss Snooty raising her voice:

'I'm afraid you've forgotten two things, dear,' she said.

'Oh dear!' thought Mrs Pepperpot, 'the cream-jug and the sugar-bowl! I shall have to look and see if they are both filled.'

The cream-jug was full, but when Mrs Pepperpot leaned over the edge of the sugar-bowl she toppled in! And at the same moment Rita rushed in, put the lid on the sugar-bowl and put it and the cream-jug on a little tray. Then she turned round and went back to the staff-room.

First Mrs Pepperpot wondered if she should tell Rita where she was, but she was afraid the child might drop the tray altogether, so instead she buried herself well down in the sugar-bowl and hoped for the best.

Rita started carrying the tray round. But her teacher hadn't finished with her yet. 'I hope you remembered the sugar-tongs,' she said.

Rita didn't know what to say, but Mrs Pepperpot heard the remark, and when the visiting head teacher took the lid off, Mrs Pepperpot popped up like a jack-in-the-box holding a lump of sugar in her outstretched hand. She stared straight in front of her and never moved an eyelid, so the head teacher didn't notice anything odd. He simply took the sugar lump and waved Rita on with the tray. But his neighbour at the table looked hard at Mrs Pepperpot and said: 'What very curious sugar-tongs – I suppose they're made of plastic.

Whatever will they think of next?' Then he asked Rita if she had brought them with her from home, and she said yes, which was strictly true, of course.

After that everyone wanted to have a look at the curious sugar-tongs, till in the end Rita's teacher called her over.

'Let me have a look at those tongs,' she said. She reached out her hand to pick them up, but this was too much for Mrs Pepperpot. In a moment she had the whole tray over and everything fell on the floor. The cream-jug was smashed and the contents of the sugar-bowl rolled under the cupboard, which was just as well for Mrs Pepperpot!

But the teacher thought it was she who had upset the tray, and suddenly she was sorry she had been so hard on the little girl. She put her arms round Rita and gave her a hug. 'It was all my fault,' she said. 'You've been a very good little parlourmaid.'

Later, when all the guests had gone, and Rita was clearing the table, the teacher pointed to the dark corner by the cupboard and said, 'Who is that standing there?'

And out stepped Mrs Pepperpot as large as life and quite unruffled. 'I've been sent to lend a hand with the washing-up,' she said. 'Give me that tray, Rita. You and I will go out into the kitchen.'

When at last the two of them were walking home, Rita said. 'Why did you help me all day when I was so horrid to you this morning?'

'Well,' said Mrs Pepperpot,' perhaps it was because you *were* so horrid. Next time maybe I'll help that Miss Snooty of yours. She looks pretty horrid too, but she might be nice underneath.

# *Mrs Pepperpot on the Warpath*

It was the day after Mrs Pepperpot had helped
Rita at the school party, and the little old woman
was in a terrible rage. You see, if there's anything
Mrs Pepperpot hates, it's people being unkind
to children. All night she had been thinking
about it, and now she had made up her mind to
go and tell Rita's teacher just what she thought
of her. So she put on her best hat and her best
frock, straightened her back and marched off to
the school.

'I hope I don't shrink this time,' she thought, 'but it's not likely to happen two days running. Anyway, today I must have my say or I shall burst. Somebody's going to say she's sorry or my name's not Pepperpot!'

She had reached the school gate and swung it open. Then she walked up to the teacher's front door and knocked twice smartly. Then she waited.

No one said, 'Come in!'

Mrs Pepperpot knocked again, but there was still no answer. So she decided to try the latch. 'If the door isn't locked I shall go straight in,' she said to herself. She pressed the latch and the door opened. But no sooner had she put a foot over the threshold than she shrank and fell head over heels into a travelling-rug which was rolled up on the floor just inside the door! Next to it stood a suitcase and a hatbox.

'Oh, calamity!' cried Mrs Pepperpot, 'let's hope she's not in after all now!' But she was unlucky, for now she could hear footsteps in the corridor and the teacher came towards the front door dressed in her going-out clothes.

'What an old dolt I am!' thought Mrs Pepperpot. 'Fancy me not remembering the summer holidays have started today and she'll be going away, of course. Oh well, she's not gone yet. If I can manage to stay near her for a little while longer I may still get my chance to give her a piece of my mind.' So she hid in the rug.

The teacher picked up the suitcase in one hand, then she threw the travelling-rug over her shoulder and picked up the hatbox in the other hand and walked out of the house, closing the door behind her. And Mrs Pepperpot? She was clinging for dear life to the fringe of the rug and she was still as angry as ever.

'Very nice, I must say!' she muttered. 'Going away on a holiday like this without a thought for Rita and all the harm you did her. But you wait, my fine lady, very soon it'll be my turn to teach you a thing or two!'

The teacher walked briskly on, with Mrs Pepperpot dangling behind her, till they got to the station. Then she walked over to the fruit-stall and put the rug down on the counter, and Mrs Pepperpot was able to slip out of it and hide behind a bunch of flowers.

The teacher asked for two pounds of apples.

'That's right!' fumed Mrs Pepperpot to herself. 'Buy two pounds of apples to gorge yourself with on the train!'

'And eight oranges, please,' continued the teacher.

'Worse and worse!' muttered Mrs Pepperpot.

'And three pounds of bananas, please,' said the teacher.

Mrs Pepperpot could hardly contain herself: 'If I was my proper size now, I'd give you apples and oranges and bananas, and no mistake!'

Then the teacher said to the lady in the fruit-stall:

'Do you think you could do me a favour? I want all this fruit to go to one of my pupils, but I have to catch the train, so I've no time to take it to her myself. Could you deliver it to Rita Johansen in the little house by the church and tell her it's from me?'

On hearing this, Mrs Pepperpot's ears nearly fell off with astonishment. It was just as if some-one had taken a sweet out of her mouth and left her nothing to suck; what was she going to say now?

'I'll do that for you with pleasure, miss,' said the fruit-lady. 'That'll be twelve shillings exactly.'

'Oh dear!' exclaimed the teacher, rummaging

in her purse, 'I see I shan't have enough money left after buying my ticket. Would you mind if I owed you the twelve shillings till I come back from my holidays?'

'The very idea! Asking me to deliver goods you can't even pay for! I shall have to have the fruit back, please,' the fruit-lady said, and held out her hand.

The teacher said she was sorry, put the bag of fruit back on the counter and went off to board her train, but Mrs Pepperpot had taken the chance to jump into the bag.

Silently she wished the teacher a good holiday: 'You're not so bad after all, and you needn't worry; I'll see that Rita gets her bag of fruit somehow. But *somebody's* going to get the edge of my tongue before the day's out!'

Of course the fruit-lady could no more hear what Mrs Pepperpot was saying than the teacher could. She was busy getting ready to shut up shop and go home. But when she had put her hat on and opened the door she suddenly turned round and picked up the bag of fruit on the counter.

Mrs Pepperpot had just been wondering if she was going to be locked in the fruit-stall all night, and now here she was, being taken on another journey!

'I suppose you're going to eat all this your-self, you selfish old thing, you!' thought Mrs Pepperpot, getting worked up again. 'The teacher may be snooty, but at least she has a kind heart underneath. You're just plain mean! But just you wait till I grow again!'

The fruit-lady walked on and on, until at last Mrs Pepperpot could hear her opening a door and going into a room. There she set the bag down with a thump on the table, and Mrs Pepperpot was able to climb over an orange and peep out of the top.

She saw a man banging on the table, and he was as cross as a sore bear. 'What sort of time is this to come home?' he roared. 'I've been waiting and waiting for my supper. Hurry up now! What's in that bag anyway?'

'Oh, it's only some fruit for a little girl,' said his wife. 'The school-teacher wanted to send it to Rita Johansen, but she found she hadn't enough money, so I took it back. Then when she'd gone I felt sorry, so I thought I'd take it along to the child myself.'

This time Mrs Pepperpot was really amazed: 'Well, I never!' she gasped, 'here's another one who turns out to be nice. Still I'm sure her husband won't; he looks as if he could do with a good ticking off!'

The fruit-lady's husband certainly was a cross-patch and no mistake. He banged his fist on the table and shouted that no wife of his was going to waste money and time running errands for silly school-teachers and brats.

'Give me that bag!' he roared. 'I'll take it right back to the shop this minute!' And he snatched up the bag from the table. Poor Mrs Pepperpot was given an awful shaking and landed up jammed between two bananas.

Taking long strides, the man walked off down the road.

'Bye-bye, fruit-lady!' whispered Mrs Pepperpot. 'You have a nasty husband, but I'll deal with him shortly, don't you worry!'

Squeezed and bruised, the little old woman lay there in the bag while the man strode on. But after a while he walked more slowly and at last he stopped at a house and knocked on the door.

'Surely this isn't the station?' wondered Mrs Pepperpot.

She heard the door open and the man spoke: 'Are you Rita Johansen?'

Then she heard a little girl's voice, 'Yes, that's me.'

'Your teacher sent you this,' said the man and handed over the bag; 'it's fruit.'

'Oh, thank you!' said Rita. 'I'll just go and get a bowl to put it in.' And she set the bag on a chair.

'That's all right,' said the man, and he turned on his heel and walked away.

When Rita came back with the bowl she thought she heard the door close, but she didn't take much notice in her eagerness to see what the teacher had sent her.

But it was actually Mrs Pepperpot who had slipped out, for she was now her usual size and she wanted time to think; it had all been so surprising and not at all what she expected. As she walked she began to hurry. For now she knew who was going to get a piece of her mind, and rightly so! Someone who made her more angry than anyone else just now!

When she got home she marched straight to the mirror. Putting her hands on her hips she glared at the little old woman she saw there. 'Well!' she said, 'and who do you think you are, running round the country-side, poking your nose in where you're not wanted? Is it any of your business, may I ask, who the school-teacher buys fruit for? What d'you mean by hiding in people's travelling-rugs and spying on them? You ought to be ashamed of yourself, an old woman like you, behaving like a senseless child. As for the fruit-lady, why shouldn't she be cross? How was she to know if she could trust the teacher? And her husband; I suppose he can bang his fist on his own table if he likes without you interfering? Are you listening? Wouldn't you be pretty mad if you'd come home hungry and the wife wasn't there to cook your meal, eh? I'm disgusted with you! *They* were sorry for what they did and made amends, all three of them, but *you*, you just stand there glaring at me as if nothing had  happened. Wouldn't it be an idea to say you were sorry?'

Mrs Pepperpot turned her back on the mirror and took a deep breath. 'That's better!' she said. 'I've got it all off my chest at last. Now I can give my tongue a rest and get on with the housework.'

But first she took one more look in the mirror, smiled shyly and bobbed a little curtsy.

'I'm sorry!' she said.

And the little old woman in the mirror smiled back at her and bobbed a little curtsy too.

# The Nature Lesson

Every morning, when Mrs Pepperpot sits at her window with her after-breakfast cup of coffee, she watches a little boy who always walks across her yard on his way to school. The boy's name is Olly and he and Mrs Pepperpot are very good friends, though not in the way grown-ups usually are friends with children. Quite often Olly rushes past Mrs Pepperpot's window without even saying 'Good Morning', because he is in such a hurry. But then Mrs Pepperpot has never even asked him his name or how old he is or what he wants for Christmas. She just watches him every morning and says to herself. 'There goes the little boy on his way to school.' As for Olly, he just glances up at her window and thinks, 'There's the old woman, drinking her coffee.'

Now with animals it is different: if Olly sees the cat sitting on Mrs Pepperpot's door-step he can't resist stopping to stroke her. He'll even sit down on the door-step and talk to her.

'Hullo, pussy,' he'll say. 'There's a lovely pussy!' And then, of course, he has to go and see the dog outside his kennel as well, in case he should get jealous.

'Hullo, boy! Good dog, good dog! You didn't think I'd forgotten you, did you? Oh, I wouldn't do that! There's a good dog!' And by the time he's made a fuss of them both he's late for school.

This is Olly's trouble: he's *very* fond of animals. He loves to play hide-and-seek with the squirrel he sees on his way to school, or to have a whistling-match with a blackbird. And as for *rainy* days, well, he spends so much time trying not to step on the worms wriggling by the puddles in the road that he's *always* late for school.

This won't do, of course, and when he's late his teacher gets cross, and she'll say, 'It's all very well being fond of animals; it's quite right that you should be, but it's no excuse for being late for school.'

But that wasn't what I was going to tell you. What I was going to tell you was how Mrs Pepperpot had a nature lesson one day. So here we go!

It was a lovely spring day, and Mrs Pepperpot was sitting by the window as usual, enjoying her cup of coffee and watching Olly come across the yard. He was walking rather briskly this time – watching some bird or animal had probably made him late again – so he had only time to say 'Hullo, puss!' to the cat on the doorstep and 'Hi, boy!' to the dog by the kennel.

But suddenly he stopped dead, turned round on his heel and started running back across the yard. Mrs Pepperpot had just come to the door to give the dog his breakfast and Olly rushed past her as fast as he could go.

Mrs Pepperpot called to him: 'Whatever's the matter with you, boy? The police after you?'

'Forgot my nature textbook!' answered Olly over his shoulder, and started off again.

'Wait a minute!' called Mrs Pepperpot. Olly stopped. 'You can't go all the way home again now; you'll be much too late for school. No, you go on and I'll go back for your book and bring it to you at school.'

Olly shuffled his feet a bit and looked unhappy; he didn't much like the idea of an old woman turning up in school with his nature textbook.

'Don't stand there shuffling, boy!' said Mrs Pepperpot. 'Where did you leave the book?'

'On the window-sill,' he answered; 'the window is open.'

'All right. Where do you want me to put the book when I get to the school? Come on, hurry up; we haven't got all day!' said Mrs Pepperpot, trying to look severe.

'There's a hole in the wall, just by the big birch tree; there's an old bird-nest there you can put it in.'

'In the old nest in a hole in the wall by the birch tree; right!' said Mrs Pepperpot. 'Now, off you go and see if you can be on time for a change! I'll see to the rest.'

'Righto!' said Olly and was off before you could say Jack Robinson.

Mrs Pepperpot took off her apron, smoothed her hair and stepped out into the yard. And then, of course, the inevitable thing happened; she shrank!

'This is bad,' thought Mrs Pepperpot, as she peeped over the wet grass by the door-step, 'but I've known worse.' She called to the cat: 'Come here, puss! You'll have to be my horse once again and help me fetch Olly's nature book from his house.'

'Miaow! All right,' said the cat, as she allowed Mrs Pepperpot to climb on her back. 'What sort of thing is a nature book?'

'It's a book the children use in school to learn about animals,' answered Mrs Pepperpot, 'and one thing it says about cats is that you are "carnivores".'

'What does that mean?' asked the cat.

'That you eat meat, but never mind that now; all you have to do is to take me straight down the road till we get to the stream. Then we take a short cut across . . .'

But, as they came near the stream, the cat said, 'Doesn't the book say anything about cats not liking to get their feet wet?' And then she stopped so abruptly that poor Mrs Pepperpot toppled right over her head and fell plump into the water!

'Good job I can swim,' spluttered Mrs Pepperpot as she came to the surface, 'humans aren't meant to live under water on account of the way they breathe with their lungs. Phew! It's hard work all the same; I'll take a rest on this stone and see if something turns up.'

While she was getting her breath a tiny animal stuck its nose out of the water, and started snarling at her. Now Mrs Pepperpot knew what that was, but you probably wouldn't, because it only lives in the faraway places, and it is called a lemming. Its fur is dappled brown and fawn, so that it looks a bit like a guinea-pig in summer, but in winter it turns white as the snow around it.

As I say, Mrs Pepperpot knew all about lemmings, so she snarled back at the little creature, making as horrible a noise as she could. 'I'm not afraid of you!' she said, 'though the book says you're the worst-tempered of all the little rodents and don't give way to a fierce dog or even a grown man. But you can just stop showing off and help me out of this stream like a good lemming.'

'Well, blow me down!' said the lemming. 'I never saw a woman as small as you with such a loud voice. Get on my back and I'll take you across. Where are you going, by the way?'

'To fetch a nature book from the house over there for a little boy at school,' said Mrs Pepperpot. 'And in that book there is quite a bit about you.'

'Oh? And what does it say?' asked the lemming, crawling out on to the grass with Mrs Pepperpot.

'It says that once every so many years lemmings come down from the mountains in great swarms and eat up all the green stuff they can find till they get to the sea.' Then she stopped, because she remembered that when the lemmings reach the sea in their search for food, thousands of them get drowned.

'We do get rather hungry,' said the lemming; 'as a matter of fact, I'm on my way now to join my mates in a little food-hunt . . .'

'Couldn't you just take me down to the house?' pleaded Mrs Pepperpot; she didn't like the idea that he might drown in the sea. But the lemming's empty tummy was telling him to go, so he told Mrs Pepperpot she would have to manage by herself, and he ran off muttering to himself about juicy green leaves.

Before Mrs Pepperpot had had time to wonder what would happen to him, another head appeared above a little wall. This time it was a stoat.

'Hullo, Mr Nosey Parker,' she greeted him, 'what are you looking for?'

'I thought you were a mouse, but I see you're a little old woman, and I don't eat women,' said the stoat. 'Have you by any chance got a silver spoon?' he added.

'I have something you like even better than silver spoons,' answered Mrs Pepperpot, 'a whole packet of tin-tacks, and you can have them if you'll take me to that house over there. I have to fetch a book from the window-sill for a little boy in the school.

'All right,' said the stoat, 'hop up!'

So Mrs Pepperpot got on his back. But it was a most uncomfortable journey, because stoats, like weasels, move by rippling their long bodies, and though they have short legs, they can run very fast. Mrs Pepperpot had a job keeping on and was glad when they reached the wall under the window.

The stoat scrambled up to the window-sill, and presently he came back with the book – under his chin.

'Why do you carry the book that way?' asked Mrs Pepperpot.

'How else?' answered the stoat. 'I always carry eggs under my chin.'

'Eggs?' Mrs Pepperpot pretended to be surprised. 'I didn't know stoats laid eggs.'

'Ha, ha, very funny!' said the stoat. 'I suppose you don't eat eggs?'

'Oh yes,' said Mrs Pepperpot, 'but I don't steal them out of wild birds' nests.'

'That's my business,' said the stoat. 'Now you'd better think how you're going to get this book to school; I can't carry both you and the book.'

'That's true!' said Mrs Pepperpot. 'I'll have to think of something.'

But it wasn't necessary, for the next moment Mrs Pepperpot was back to her proper size. As she bent down to pick up the book she whispered to the little stoat, 'The tin-tacs will be waiting for you in that nest you robbed in the stone wall by the school.' And she thought she heard him chuckle as he rippled away in the grass.

When she reached the school the bell was ringing for break, and she just had time to pop the book into the empty nest before Olly came running out with the other children. Mrs Pepperpot gave the tiniest nod in the direction of the wall and then she walked briskly away.

But the next morning Olly brought a lovely bone for her dog and from his milk bottle he poured a good saucer-full of milk for her pussy.

Mrs Pepperpot opened the window. 'Would you do something for me this morning?' she asked.

'As long as it won't make me late for school,' answered Olly.

'Good,' said Mrs Pepperpot. Then she fetched a packet of tin-tacks from the toolshed and gave them to Olly. 'Put those in the empty nest in the wall, will you? They're for a friend of mine.'

# The Shoemaker's Doll

There was once a shoemaker who won a doll
in a raffle at a bazaar. But a doll was no good
to him, living alone as he did in a little cottage
where the floor was strewn with old soles and
bits of leather and where everything he touched
was covered in glue.

The shoemaker pushed his spectacles up on his forehead and stared at the woman. Then he said, 'Come again Tuesday!'

'But it's Tuesday today,' objected the woman.

The shoemaker let his spectacles fall back on his nose.

'Come again Wednesday!' he snapped and went on with his work.

'Oh, you're just the same old lazy sour-puss that you always were!' said the woman, and left him to it.

In the afternoon a little boy started playing in the street outside the house. He came to the door and asked the shoemaker to button his jacket because his fingers were too cold to manage the buttonhole.

'Come again Thursday!' said the shoemaker in his snappy voice.

'But I'm cold today, mister!' said the little boy.

'Come again Friday!' said the shoemaker.

'You're just a grumpy old toad, so you are!' said the little boy, and went away.

'Good riddance!' said the shoemaker, and he didn't even turn round, but went on with his work, mending and patching till it was too dark to work any more. Then he ate up the rest of

the loaf and climbed into bed. But in his sleep
he dreamed that the doll came over to him and
this is what she said:

'I can button, mend a hose,
I can wipe a runny nose,
If *you* won't, I will!'

'You're a proper fusspot, aren't you?' said the
shoemaker when he woke in the morning and
remembered his dream. 'I'd better get those
shoes finished for Mrs Butt. Then when I take
them along to her I can take the ring for the
little girl as well.'

So he sat down at his
bench and finished mending
Mrs Butt's shoes.

Meanwhile the little boy
had started playing outside
the window again; the
shoemaker called him in.

'Come here, boy, let me
button your coat for you,'
he said. 'Would you like me
to wipe that nose of yours
too? You can tell me if it
hurts.'

'Course it doesn't hurt,' said the little boy, blowing into the hankie like a trumpet and waving his fingers in the air; they were quite stiff and blue with cold. 'Not so cross today, are you?' he said, and then he added: 'I'd like to help *you* now. Got any messages for me to take?'

'Well yes, I have, as a matter of fact,' said the shoemaker. 'You can take these shoes to Mrs Butt at the corner, and while you're at it you can take this ring and give it to the little girl at Cragg House; she lost it here a long time ago.'

'All right!' said the little boy and ran off with the things.

It wasn't long before he was back with a message from Mrs Butt. 'Mrs Butt told me to tell you that if you want your Sunday suit cleaned and pressed she'd be glad to do it for you. And that girl at Crag House told me to thank you and ask if you'd like to go to her birthday party tomorrow – she's asked me too, wasn't that nice of her?'

The shoemaker was staring in front of him, thinking hard. 'Very nice of her, I'm sure. But, as for me, I've been on my own for so long now I wouldn't know how to behave with other folks at a party. No, I'd better not go.'

But when the little boy had gone away and

the shoemaker had got into bed he dreamed
again that the doll came over to speak to him:

> 'I always smile when folks are kind,
> Not turn my back and act so blind,
> If *you* won't, I will!'

Next morning the shoemaker
remembered and said to himself,
'I shall have to go, then.' And he
has never regretted it. For one
thing, he wore his Sunday suit, all
neatly cleaned and pressed by Mrs
Butt, and, for another, he had three
different kinds of cake to eat, and,
most important of all, he found
out that it is good for people to
get together now and then and not
always to be moping on their own.

Ever since that day the shoemaker's cottage
has been as clean as a new pin, and the shoemaker
himself whistles and sings as he goes about his
housework. He makes his bed and scrubs the
floor, he buttons boys' coats and wipes their
noses and he mends the shoes in double-quick
time.

Every now and again, when there's something

he *doesn't* want to do, he takes a quick look at his doll on the chest of drawers, and he always ends up by doing whatever it is he has to do. For if *he* won't, *she* will.

# Mrs Pepperpot is Taken
## for a Witch

Mrs Pepperpot lives in a valley in Norway, and in summertime in that part of the world the nights hardly get dark at all. On Midsummer's Eve, in fact, the sun never quite goes down, so everybody, young and old, stays up all night to dance and sing and let off fireworks round a big bonfire. And because there's magic abroad on Midsummer's Eve they sometimes see witches riding on broomsticks through the sky – or they think they do, anyway.

Now the only two people in that valley who never used to go to the bonfire party were Mr and Mrs Pepperpot. Not that Mrs Pepperpot didn't want to go, but Midsummer's Eve happened to be Mr Pepperpot's birthday as well, and on that day it was he who decided what they did. He never liked mixing with a crowd on account of that shrinking habit of Mrs Pepperpot; he was always afraid that she would suddenly turn the size of a pepperpot and disappear, leaving him standing there looking a proper fool.

But this year Mrs Pepperpot *did* go to the party, and this is how it happened.

It started the night before Midsummer's Eve. Mrs Pepperpot had been to the store and was walking slowly home with her basket on her arm. She was wondering how she could persuade her husband to go to the bonfire when suddenly she had an idea.

'I could ask him if there was something he really wanted for his birthday, and then I could say I would give it to him if he promised to take me to the bonfire party.'

As soon as she got inside the door she jumped on her husband's knee and gave him a smacking kiss on the tip of his nose.

'Dear, good hubby,' she said, 'have you got a very special wish for your birthday tomorrow?'

Her husband was quite surprised. 'Have you had sun-stroke or something? How could you buy anything? Why, money runs through your fingers like water.'

'Sometimes it does, and sometimes it doesn't,' said Mrs Pepperpot, looking sly; 'there are such things as hens, and hens lay eggs and eggs can be sold. Just now I have quite a tidy sum put by, so just you tell me what you would like and the present will be laid out here on the table as sure as my name's Pepperpot.'

'Well,' he said, 'if you think you have enough money to buy that handsome pipe with the silver band that's lying in the store window, I'll promise you something in return.'

'Done!' cried Mrs Pepperpot at once, 'and the thing I want you to promise me is to take me to the bonfire party on Windy Ridge tomorrow night!'

So Mr Pepperpot had to agree and the next day Mrs Pepperpot filled her pockets with all the sixpennies, pennies and threepenny bits she had earned from the eggs and set off to the store.

'I want to buy the pipe with the silver band,'

said Mrs Pepperpot, when it came to her turn to be served.

But the grocer shook his head. 'Sorry, Mrs Pepperpot,' he said, 'but I'm afraid I sold that pipe to Peter Poulsen yesterday.'

'Oh dear,' said Mrs Pepperpot, 'I'll have to go and see if he'll let me buy it off him,' and she hurried out of the door, letting the door-bell jingle loudly as she went.

She took the shortest way to Peter Poulsen's house, but when she got there only his wife was at home.

'I was wondering if your husband would sell me that pipe he bought in the store yesterday?' said Mrs Pepperpot. 'I'd pay him well for it,' she added, and patted her pocketful of coins.

'That pipe is no longer in the house,' said Mrs Poulsen, who had a sour look on her face. 'I wasn't going to have tobacco smoke in my curtains, no *thank* you! I gave it to some boys who were having a sale; they said they were collecting money for fireworks for tonight's bonfire, or some such nonsense.'

Mrs Pepperpot's heart sank; did Mrs Poulsen know where the sale was being held?

'Up on Windy Ridge, near the bonfire, the boys said,' answered Mrs Poulsen, and Mrs Pepperpot lost no time in making her way up to Windy Ridge.

But it was a tidy walk uphill and when she got to the top she found the boys had sold everything. They were busy tidying up the bits of paper and string and cardboard boxes and carrying them over to the bonfire.

Mrs Pepperpot was so out of breath her tongue was hanging out, but she managed to stammer, 'Who got the pipe?'

'What pipe?' asked one of the boys.

'The one with the silver band that Mrs

Poulsen gave you.'

'Oh that,' said the boy; 'my brother bought it. But then he tried to smoke it and it made him sick. So he got fed up with it and tied it to a long pole and stuck it at the top of the bonfire. There it is – look!'

Mrs Pepperpot looked, and there it was, right enough, tied to a pole at the very top of the huge bonfire!

'Couldn't you take it down again?' she asked the boy.

'Are you crazy?' said the boy. 'Expect us to upset the bonfire when we've got everything piled up just nicely? Not likely! Besides, we're going to have some fun with that pipe;

you wait and see! But I can't stand talking now, I must go and get a can of petrol to start it off.' And he ran off with the other boys.

'Oh dear, oh dear, oh dear!' wailed Mrs Pepperpot to herself. 'I see there's nothing for it but to climb that bonfire and get it down myself.' But she looked with dismay at the mountain of old mattresses, broken chairs, table-legs, barrows, drawers, old clothes and hats, car-tyres and empty cartons.

'First I shall have to find a stick to poke the pipe off the pole when I do get up aloft,' she thought.

Just at that moment she turned small, but for once Mrs Pepperpot was really pleased. 'Hooray!' she shouted in her shrill little voice. 'It won't take long for a little thing like me to get that pipe down now, and I don't even need to upset the bonfire!'

Quick as a mouse, she darted into the big pile and started climbing up from the inside. But it was not as easy as she thought; climbing over a mattress she got her heel stuck in a spring and it took her quite a while to free herself. Then she had difficulty in climbing a slippery chair-leg; she kept sliding back. But at last she managed it, only to find herself entangled in the lining of a coat. She groped about in this for some time before she found her way out of the sleeve.

By now people had started gathering round the bonfire.

'All right, let them have a good look,' she thought. 'Luckily I'm too small for them to see me up here. And nothing's going to stop me from getting to the top now!'

Just then she lost her grip and fell into a deep drawer. There she lay, puffing and blowing, till she managed to catch hold of a bonnet string which was hanging over the edge of the drawer.

'Not much further to go, thank goodness!' she told herself, but when she looked down she almost fainted; it was fearfully far to the ground, and now there were crowds of people standing around, waiting for the bonfire to be lit.

'No time to lose!' thought Mrs Pepperpot, and heaved herself on to the last obstacle. This was easy, because it was an old concertina, so she could walk up it like a staircase.

Now she was at the foot of the pole and at the top was the pie, securely tied!

'However am I going to get up there?' she wondered, but then she noticed the rim of an empty tar-barrel right next to her. So she

smeared a little tar on her hands to give them a better grip, and then she started to climb the pole. But the pole and the whole bonfire seemed to be heeling a little over to one side, and when she looked down she nearly fell off with fright: *the boys had lit the bonfire!*

Little flames were licking up round the mattresses and the broken furniture.

Then people started cheering and the children chanted: 'Wait till it gets to the pipe at the top! Wait till it gets to the pipe at the top!'

'Catch me waiting!' muttered Mrs Pepperpot. 'I've got to get there *first!*' and she climbed on up till her hands gripped the stem of the pipe. Down below she could hear the children shouting:

'Watch the flames when they reach the pole! There's a rocket tied to the pipe!'

'Oh, good gracious!' cried Mrs Pepperpot, clinging on for dear life. BANG! Up into the cold night sky shot the rocket, the pole, the pipe *and* Mrs Pepperpot!

Round the bonfire everyone suddenly stopped shouting. A thin woman in a shawl whispered to her neighbour:

'I thought I saw something sitting on that stick!'

Her neighbour, who was even thinner and wore two shawls, whispered back, 'It would have been a witch!' and they both shuddered. But from behind them came a man's voice:

'Oh, it couldn't be her, could it?' It was Mr Pepperpot who had just left off working and had taken a ride up to the mountain to have a look at the bonfire. Now he swung himself on his bicycle again and raced home as fast as he could go, muttering all the way, 'Let her be at home; oh, please let her be at home!' When he reached the house and opened the door his hand was shaking.

There stood Mrs Pepperpot, quite her normal size and with no sign of a broomstick. She was decorating his birthday cake and on the table, neatly laid on a little cloth, was the precious pipe with its silver band.

'Many Happy Returns of the Day!' said Mrs Pepperpot. 'Come and have your meal now. Then you can put on a clean shirt and take your wife to dance all night at the bonfire party!'

'Anything you say!' said Mr Pepperpot; he was so relieved she hadn't gone off with the witches of Midsummer's Eve.

# *The Little Mouse Who was*
# *Very Clever*

There was once a little mouse called Squeak, who sat behind the door in his mousehole, waiting for his mother to come home from the larder with some food.

Suddenly there was a knock at the door.

'Who is that?' asked little Squeak.

'Peep, peep, let me in, it's your mother,' said a voice outside, but it didn't sound a mousy sort of voice.

'Why are you knocking at our door?'

'I forgot to take the key,' said the voice.

'We don't use a key for this door,' said the little mouse. 'It's bolted on the inside and I'm not opening it for *you*!'

Whoever it was went away and Squeak waited for some time before there came another knock.

'Who is that?' asked Squeak.

'It's Peter,' said a voice, but it didn't sound like Peter, the little boy who lived in the house.

'Why are you knocking at our door?'

'Because you've been using my shawl for your bed,' said the voice.

'If you're a little boy, you won't want a shawl,' said Squeak. 'I'm not opening the door for you!'

After he had waited some time there was another knock.

'Who is that?' he asked.

'Peter's mother,' came the reply; 'let me in.'

'Why are you knocking at our door?'

'Because I think you must have hidden my braces down your hole,' said the voice, which sounded rather purry for a lady.

'If you are Peter's mother,' said little Squeak, 'I'm sure you don't need braces. I'm not opening the door for *you*!'

Again he had to wait a long time before the next knock.

'Who is that?' said Squeak.

'This is Peter's father,' said a voice that was very croaky. 'Let me in at once!'

'Why are you knocking at our door?' asked the little mouse.

'My tail went in the honey-pot and I want you to clean it.'

'If you are Peter's father,' said Squeak, 'why have you got a tail? I'm not opening the door for *you*!'

After that there was a long, long silence, and then at last there was a tiny little knock.

'Who is that?' asked Squeak.

'It's your mother, darling.'

But the little mouse wanted to make quite sure:

'Why are you knocking at our door?'

'Because I want my clever Squeak to unbolt

it as he always does,' said the voice. Then he knew it was his mother, and the little mouse, who was too clever to be tricked by a cat with many voices, unbolted the door and let his mother in.

And because he'd been so clever his mother gave him an extra large lump of cheese for his supper.

# Mrs Pepperpot's Birthday

It was Mrs Pepperpot's birthday, so she had asked her neighbours in to coffee at three o'clock. All day she had been scrubbing and polishing, and now it was ten minutes to three and she was putting the final touches to the strawberry layer cake on the kitchen table. As she stood balancing the last strawberry on a spoon, she suddenly felt herself shrinking, not slowly as she sometimes did, but so fast that she didn't even have time to put the strawberry on a plate. It rolled on to the floor and Mrs Pepperpot tumbled after it. But she quickly picked herself up and jumped into the cat's basket. Puss was a bit surprised, but allowed her to snuggle down with the kittens. In her black–and–white striped skirt and white blouse, she hoped the guests would take her for one of the cat-family, until the magic wore off and she could be her real size again. For you may remember that Mrs Pepperpot never liked anyone to see her when she was tiny.

There was a knock at the door, and, when it wasn't answered, Sarah from South Farm walked into the little front hall, carrying a huge bunch of lilac.

'Many Happy Returns of the Day!' said Sarah. There was no reply, so she peered into the kitchen, thinking Mrs Pepperpot might be in there, though, naturally, she didn't look in the cat-basket. Somehow she managed to knock over the flower-vase on the hall table, and the water spilled on the tablecloth and on to the floor.

'Oh dear, oh dear!' thought Sarah. 'I shall have to mop that up before anybody notices.'

But at that moment there was another knock at the door. So Sarah ran into the kitchen and hid in a cupboard.

In came Norah from North Farm, and she was carrying a very nice tablecloth.

'Many Happy Returns!' she said, but, as she got no answer, she looked round for Mrs Pepperpot, and her parcel swept the vase off the table on to the floor.

'That's bad!' thought Norah. 'I must put it back before anybody comes.'

But before she could do it there was another knock on the door and Norah hurried into the bedroom and crept under the bed.

Esther from East Farm came in, carrying a handsome glass bowl for Mrs Pepperpot. When she had said 'Many Happy Returns!' and no one answered, she walked straight into the living-room. Carrying the bowl in front of her, she didn't notice the vase on the floor and put her foot straight on it. There was a nasty crunch and there it lay, in smithereens!

'Goodness gracious, what have I done?' thought Esther. 'Perhaps if I hide behind this curtain no one will know who did it!' So she quickly wrapped herself in one of the curtains.

At that moment the clock struck three, and the magic wore off; there was Mrs Pepperpot as large as life, walking through the kitchen. 'Coo-ee!' she called. 'You can all come out now!'

So Sarah stepped out of the cupboard, Norah crawled from under the bed, while Esther unwrapped herself from the curtain in the living-room.

At first they looked a bit sheepish, but then they said 'Many Happy Returns!' all over again and they had a good laugh, while Mrs Pepperpot swept up the broken vase, threw away the dead flowers and put the wet tablecloth in the wash-tub.

Then she thanked them for their fine presents; the table was spread with Norah's tablecloth, Esther's glass bowl was filled with fresh water, and the huge bunch of lilac that Sarah had brought was put into it.

After that Mrs Pepperpot brought in the coffee and cakes and they all sat down to enjoy themselves. But on the strawberry layer cake there was one strawberry missing.

'You see,' said Mrs Pepperpot, when they asked her what had happened to it, 'my first visitor this afternoon was the little old woman who shrinks, and she was so tiny today that one strawberry was all she could manage to eat. So I gave her that and a thimble of milk to wash it down.'

'Didn't you ask her to stay, so that we could see her?' asked Sarah, for they were all very curious about the little old woman who shrank, and nobody thereabouts had ever seen her.

'She was sorry, she said, but she was in a tearing hurry; she had some business with a mouse, her night watchman or something. But she told me to tell you she did enjoy our little game of hide-and-seek!'

# The Dancing Bees

You have probably been told that bees are very busy, hardworking creatures, collecting honey from the flowers from morning till night all through the summer to store it up for food in winter.

But now you shall hear about a she-bee who spent her time in quite a different way; she did nothing but dance. And what gave her this curious idea? Well, wait till I tell you.

One evening in June this she-bee was on her way home to the hive from the meadows, but she hadn't found any honey that day. So when she saw a beautiful flower right below her she swooped down and settled on it. But the flower was swinging round because it was fixed to a hat, and the hat was on the head of a girl, and the girl was dancing with her young man to the band in People's Park.

At first the little she-bee was disappointed to find no honey in the flower, but soon she forgot

all about it; it was such a delicious feeling to sway up and down in time to the music.

'It's like hearing a thousand bumble-bees humming over a field of clover,' she murmured happily as she swayed round and round.

'Yes, isn't it?' said a voice quite close to her. And there, on the boy's hat, sat another bee!

'I shouldn't talk to strangers, I know,' said the little she-bee, 'but this music is making me so giddy I don't really know what I'm doing.'

'Nothing wrong in talking, surely?' said the other bee, who was, of course, a he-bee. 'Allow me to say that you dance superbly, and it's not easy to hang on to a flower that is swinging round and round. I know what I'm talking about; there were two young lady bees here earlier this summer and I tried to dance with them, but they both fell off after just a few turns. I always hold on to the young man's hat-brim; in any case, this is my second season here, so I've had plenty of practice. Ah, the music is stopping; that means it's time for refreshments. Just stay where you are.'

The girl and the young man moved over to the refreshment tent and the bees went with them on their hats.

'Do you live far from here?' asked the he-bee.

'It's quite a long flight,' said the she-be, 'but I simply daren't let anyone see me home, as we have such a very strict doorkeeper.'

'I quite understand,' he replied, 'but perhaps you will permit me to fetch you a little drink of fruit juice?'

He flew down on to the table and a moment later brought back a drop of fruit-juice on one of his wings. 'Excuse my wing, but it is the only way I can manage it.'

'Very nice of you to bother; thank you very much,' said the little she-bee. 'Aren't you having any yourself?'

'Not for me, thanks, I'm driving – at least, it's not exactly *me* driving, but I daren't take any risks, all the same. I shall have to get back to my own hat now, I see they're starting the show.'

The little she-bee would have liked to ask what a 'show' was, but she felt shy, so she just rubbed her wings with her feet.

'Tonight there's a fellow with a guitar – forgotten his name, but he's very famous,' the he-bee told her. 'One young lady bee told me she once sat on his guitar while he played "Rocking round the Clock", and she'll never forget it as long as she lives, she said.'

The little she-bee listened while the man

on the platform sang and played his guitar, and very funny he looked. First he sang quite quietly, but suddenly he went into shrieks and sobs and then he fell right down on his knees and shuffled off the platform backwards.

'What happened? Did a bee sting him?' asked the she-bee.

'No, no, that was the high spot,' answered her new friend.

'The high spot? Oh yes, I've heard that high spots can sting very badly – the poor man!' And the little she-bee felt quite sorry for the man. But then the music began once more. 'Isn't it wonderful!' she cried, and clapped her front pair of feet.

They sailed out on the dance-floor again, she on her flower and he on his hat brim.

'I'm afraid that's the last dance tonight,' he said. 'I can see they're beginning to put out the lights.'

'How sad! I shall have to hurry home now,' said the little she-bee, 'but thank you so much for a lovely evening.'

'You're welcome! Perhaps we could meet another time?'

'That would be very nice,' she answered.

When she got back to the hive the doorkeeper

would not let her in at first because she had no honey with her. But in the end he relented.

Next evening she went dancing again. But this time she was careful to hide a little honey in a tree-stump close to the hive, so that she could pick it up on her way home after the dance.

The he-bee on his hat-brim was very pleased to see her. 'I've been thinking about you all day,' he said.

'Very kind of you, I'm sure,' she said, looking very demure.

Like the evening before, there was music, there was dancing, the he-bee brought her fruit-juice, and then there was the show. Afterwards he persuaded her to take a little ride in the young man's car, but when the he-bee asked if he might sit on *her* hat the little she-bee said firmly, 'No.'

Later, when she got back to the hive, she had no difficulty in getting past the doorkeeper, as she had remembered her store of honey in the tree-stump.

And so it went on every evening all through the summer, and no one in the hive knew anything about it. But one day, while the she-bee was flying round looking for honey, she forgot herself; instead of her ordinary buzzing song she started to sing 'Waltzing Matilda'.

'Whatever are you buzzing?' asked the bee who was flying nearest to her.

The little she-bee got quite confused. 'It's – it's only a little waltz tune I heard,' she stammered. Then, of course, she had to explain where she had heard it. But this was just as well, for she could not have kept the secret to herself much longer.

As the day went on other bees kept flying up to her wanting her to tell them about the dancing, the music and the show, and about her dancing partner on the hat-brim.

'Can't you take us along with you tonight?' they all pleaded.

'Not tonight,' she said, 'but perhaps tomorrow, if my partner gives his permission.'

That evening was as delightful as all the rest, but the young man didn't have his car with him, so he and the girl and the bees all went for a walk in the wood instead.

'It is really just as pleasant, don't you think, to go for a walk on such a lovely evening?' said the he-bee. 'And if I'm not mistaken we're heading for that little bank with the bluebells on it.' He was right; the young man and the girl sat down

on the flowery bank, and so did the two bees.

The young man spoke softly to the girl, and she bent her head so far forward that the bee had to hold on tight not to fall off the flower.

'Why does she bend her head like that?' she asked.

'He is proposing to her,' said the he-bee. 'You had better let me come over and hold you so you don't fall off.' And he took off from the hat-brim and made an elegant landing on the flower. Then he put his wing protectingly round the little she-bee. This time she did not protest.

'What does "propose" mean?' she asked, though deep inside she had a feeling she knew what it meant already.

'He is asking if she will be his wife and stay with him for ever.'

'Oh, how wonderful!' cried the little she-bee before she could stop herself.

'Do you really think so? Then I shall propose to you this very minute,' said the he-bee, 'even though this isn't the usual way for bees to behave, I'm sure. But it's difficult, you will agree, not to be carried away in these beautiful surroundings and hearing so much love-talk!'

'Oh yes!' sighed the little she-bee, and hung

her head bashfully just like the young girl.

The next day there was a terrific hullabaloo in the hive. The bees who knew about the dancing had told a lot more bees, and now it had all got round the hive. There they were, a great black swarm of them, thronging round the entrance, all demanding to go to People's Park like the little she-bee.

'Show us the way!' they kept crying. 'Show us the way and we'll follow you!'

The little she-bee hesitated at first, but then she said: 'All right, I will. You can all come with me.' Secretly she was longing for the music and for her partner in the park.

So the whole swarm rose in the air and flew off after the she-bee. But this was in the middle of the day and there was not a soul to be seen in People's Park when they got there. No sign of the flower on the hat, or, for that matter, of the girl and the young man and the he-bee. The she-bee was lost and she knew it, but she couldn't stop now.

On, on she flew, and the swarm after her, over fields and meadows, over roads and hedges, until quite suddenly the little she-bee caught sight of something hanging on the branch of an apple tree.

It was the hat with the flower on it! She was saved!

'Come on, all of you!' she buzzed as loudly as she could. She flew to the flower and clung there. And all the other bees clung to her, till they looked like a huge black cluster of grapes shining in the sunshine.

Someone came into the orchard; it was the girl. When she saw what was happening to her hat she gave a shriek of alarm. She shouted out to someone inside the house, and out came the young man with a great big net. He put it carefully over the swarm of bees and carried it over to an empty hive. There he shook the net so that they all tumbled in, and then he put the lid on firmly.

As luck would have it, the he-bee was still perched on the young man's hat-brim, so he was able to slip into the hive with the rest of them.

After they had time to settle down in their new home the bees made the little she-bee their queen. But, from what I've heard, she was not a bit kind to the he-bee when he became her husband. And if he or any of the other bees ever dared to dream about going dancing in People's Park they soon discovered that it was the queen who called the tune from now on; their dancing days were over for good.

# How the King Learned to
# Eat Porridge

There was once a king who was wise and good and mighty and rich, but he had one fault. Not a very big fault, mind you, but annoying enough. And do you know what it was?

*He would not eat porridge.*

Now this wouldn't have mattered so much if he had kept it to himself. After all, a king has so many other things to eat. But he was an honest king, so he could not lie, and he told both the government and the people that he did not like porridge.

'I detest porridge!' he declared. 'It tastes of glue and tufts of wool. Ugh!'

And when the people of his realm heard that they wouldn't eat porridge either. They wanted to be like the king – especially the children, who thought it was wonderful not to eat porridge, and whooped with delight. On the national flag-day they walked in the procession carrying

big banners saying 'Long Live the King! Down with Porridge!'

But far up the mountains there lived a peasant with his daughter, and they had only one tiny field of their own. On this field they grew oats, and their whole livelihood depended on it. So when everyone stopped buying oats they made less and less money.

'This can't go on!' said the peasant's daughter one day. 'People not eating porridge like this. I shall have to go to the palace and give that stupid king a piece of my mind!'

'Take care, my child, you might make the king angry,' said her father.

'He'd better take care himself,' she answered, 'or *I* might get angry.' And she slung a bag of oatmeal over her shoulder and set off for the palace.

In the palace garden she met a man, but the country girl did not know he was really the king.

'Where are you off to?' asked the man.

'I'm going to the palace to teach the king to eat porridge,' she answered.

This made the man laugh. 'If you can do that,' he said, 'you're a very clever girl!' Then he went into the royal kitchen and told the royal cook that he could take a day off, as a country girl had come to town to teach him, the king, to eat porridge.

Next day, when the king was at breakfast, the peasant's daughter brought in a big steaming bowl of porridge. She was a little taken aback when she saw who the man was she had spoken to in the garden. But the king smiled at her and said:

'Come along now, you must teach me to eat this porridge of yours.'

'Oh no,' she said, 'not after making such a fool of myself, I couldn't. Anyway, I don't suppose you even know which hand to hold the spoon in?'

'I think I do,' said the king, and picked up the spoon in his right hand.

'Just as I thought!' said the girl. 'Never in all my life have I seen anyone eat porridge with the right hand!'

'All right,' said the king. 'I'll try with my left hand.'

'That's better,' said the girl, 'but I've never seen anyone with a bowl of porridge on the table while they sat on a chair to eat it. Get up on the table and put the bowl on the chair in the proper manner!'

The king was beginning to enjoy himself. First he got up on the table and then he tried to set the bowl on the chair. But this was not so easy; he nearly lost his balance several times before he managed it.

'There, now you can start eating,' said the girl.

The king held the spoon in his left hand and

bent down to the bowl. It was awkward, but he succeeded at last in getting a spoonful up to his mouth and swallowing it.

'Just a minute,' said the girl, 'you have to hold your left ear with your right hand while you're eating.'

'I expect I can manage that too,' said the king, and balanced another spoonful up to his mouth.

'That's only two spoonfuls,' she said. 'Wait till you get to the bottom of the bowl; that's when it gets really difficult.'

'Don't worry, I'll do it!' said the king, and, do

you know, he didn't give in till he had scraped the bowl clean!

'There you are!' he shouted proudly.

'There you are yourself!' said the girl. 'Now I have taught the king to eat porridge!'

At first the king was a little put out that she had tricked him in this way. But then he had to laugh.

'You're a very cunning little girl,' he said. 'I almost think I'll marry you – that is, if you're willing?'

'I might as well,' said the girl.

So they were married, and at the wedding a huge pot of hot, steaming porridge was set up in the middle of the market place, and the king commanded his people, including the whole court and all his ministers, to come and learn how to eat porridge.

The queen stood on a high tribune to teach them, and they all laughed and enjoyed themselves like anything. But when they had had their lesson the queen said:

'Now I know you can all eat porridge; so from this day on you may sit on your chairs and put your porridge bowls on the table and eat it the way you do any other food.'

But many people, especially the children, preferred the way the queen had taught them and went on doing it – secretly.

## Mrs Pepperpot Turns
### Fortune-Teller

Every morning when Mr Pepperpot goes off to work Mrs Pepperpot stands at the window and watches him till he disappears round the bend to the main road. Then she settles down in the chair by the kitchen table, picks up her empty coffee cup and starts reading her fortune in it.

Now you probably didn't know that Mrs Pepperpot could read fortunes in a cup. Well, she can; she can tell from the way the coffee grounds lie what road she will take that day and whether she will meet joy or sorrow before nightfall. Sometimes she sees the shape of a heart in the cup and that means she will have a new sweetheart. But that makes Mrs Pepperpot laugh, for to her it means she will probably get a new pet to look after – perhaps a poor little bird with a broken wing or a stray kitten on her doorstep, getting tamer and tamer as it laps up the food and milk she gives it.

But if the grounds form a cross she knows she must watch her step, for that means she will break something; it could be when she is washing up or when she is scrubbing the floor. If she sees a clear drop of coffee running down the side of the cup that means she will hurt herself in some way and will need not only a bandage but maybe a doctor as well. And so it goes on; there are many more signs that she can read, but she only does it for herself, never for other people, even if they ask her. It's just an amusement, she says, something to while away the time when she is home alone all day.

Well, this day – it was a Friday too – Mrs Pepperpot had planned to give the house a good clean out and then she was going to bake a cake for Mr Pepperpot. Apart from that she was just going to take it easy for a change. So, when she had watched her husband turn the corner, she picked up their two coffee cups and was just about to put them in the sink. But then she stopped herself.

'There, what am I doing? I nearly forgot to have a look at my fortune for today!' So she took one of the cups back to the table and sat down. 'Let's see, now,' she said and turned the cup round and round in her hand. 'Oh dear, oh dear!' she exclaimed, 'what's this I see? A big cross? I shall have to mind how I go today and no mistake!'

At that very moment she shrank, and in no time at all she was no bigger than the coffee cup and both she and the cup fell off the chair on to the floor.

'That was a bit of a come-down!' she said, and felt both her arms and her legs to see if

there were any bones broken. But when she found she was still all in one piece she lay still for a moment, not daring to look at the cup. For it was one of her best ones, and she was sure it must have been broken by the fall.

At last she said to herself, 'I suppose I shall have to have a look.' And when she did she found to her great surprise that the cup was not even cracked or chipped.

But she was still worried. 'If that isn't it there'll be something else for me to break today,' she said miserably as she squatted down to look into the cup, for it was lying on its side.

'Oh me, oh my!' she cried. 'If this isn't my unlucky day!' she caught sight of a large clear drop on the side of the cup. 'This means tears, but I wonder what will make me cry?'

Suddenly there was a loud BANG! inside the kitchen cupboard. Mrs Pepperpot nearly jumped out of her skin with fright.

'There! Now isn't that just like Mr P., setting a mouse-trap in the cupboard, although he knows it's not necessary now that I have a mouse for a night watchman. It's only now and again that a baby mouse gets into the cupboard by mistake – before he's learned the mouse rules. It's not as if they *mean* to do any damage, so it's silly to take any notice. I wonder if I dare open the door a little to see what's happened? I suppose I'd better; the little thing might just have caught its tail and I could free it. But, of course, it might be worse than that; the cup said tears, and tears it will be, no doubt!'

So Mrs Pepperpot went over to the cupboard and pulled gently at the door. But she closed her eyes to keep back the tears which were ready to come at any moment. When she had the door opened enough to look in she opened first one eye, then the other, and then she flopped down on the floor, clapping her hands on her knees, and burst out laughing.

Right enough, the trap had snapped, but there was nothing in it. Instead two baby mice were happily playing just beside it with two empty cotton-reels. Mrs Pepperpot thought it was the funniest sight she'd ever seen.

'Hullo, Mrs Pepperpot!' squealed one of the baby mice. 'Have you shrunk again?'

'We hoped you would!' said the other one,

''cos my brother and I had never seen you small before, and Granny said we could come in here and have a peep – just in case you shrunk. We weren't being naughty – just playing cars – and then we bumped into that nasty thing which went snap over there.'

'Will you play with us?' asked the first little mouse. 'You sit in the car and we'll pull you along.'

And when Mrs Pepperpot looked closer she saw that the baby mice had fixed a matchbox over the cotton-reels and the whole contraption really moved.

'Let's go!' shouted Mrs Pepperpot, and jumped into the box.

So they played at cars, taking turns to sit in the matchbox, and Mrs Pepperpot laughed while the baby mice squealed with delight, till, all of a sudden, they heard a scratching sound above them.

'That's enough, children!' called granny mouse, whose head had appeared in a hole in the back wall. 'The cat's on top of the cupboard and the door is open!'

Before you could say 'knife' the two baby mice had disappeared through the hole, squeaking 'Thanks for the game!' as they went.

'Thank you!' said Mrs Pepperpot, and stepped out of the cupboard to see what the cat was up to.

There she was, standing on top of the cupboard waving her tail expectantly when Mrs Pepperpot came out. But Mrs Pepperpot was not standing any nonsense; she shouted at the cat: 'What are you doing up there? You get down at once or I'll teach you a lesson as soon as I grow again! Maybe it's you who are going to break something for me today? Yes, I can feel it in my bones. I know if I have another look in that cup there'll be more calamity there for me.'

By now she was just as worked up as she had been before her little game with the mice. But she couldn't resist having another look in the cup. 'Goodness gracious!' she cried. 'It's just as I thought, doctor and bandages, ambulances and everything! As if I hadn't trouble enough already! Down you get, cat, and make it quick!'

'All right! Keep your hair on,' said the cat. 'I was only doing my duty when I heard a suspicious noise in the cupboard. I'm coming down now.'

'Mind how you go! Be careful! I don't want anything broken. I'll stand here below and direct you,' said Mrs Pepperpot.

'Anybody would think I'd never jumped off a cupboard before, and I'm not in the habit of breaking things,' answered the cat, as he made his way gingerly past a big china bowl. But just on the edge of the cupboard lay a large pair of scissors, and neither the cat nor Mrs Pepperpot had seen them.

Mrs Pepperpot was busy with her warnings: 'Mind that bowl!' she shouted, standing right beneath those scissors.

The cat was being as careful as she could, but her tail brushed against the scissors, sending them flying, point downwards, to the floor. There they stood quivering!

Mrs Pepperpot had just managed to jump out of the way, but now she was too frightened to move. 'So that was it!' she stammered at last. She felt herself all over again, for this time she was *sure* she must be hurt. But she couldn't find

as much as a scratch!

A moment later she was her normal size. So she pulled the scissors out of the floor and lifted the cat down out of harm's way. Then she set to work cleaning the house and just had time to bake her cake before she heard her husband at the door.

But what a state he was in! The tears were pouring out of his eyes because of the bitter wind outside, and anyway he had a bad cold. One hand he was holding behind his back: he had fallen off his bicycle, had broken his cycle lamp and cut his hand on the glass!

As she hurriedly searched for something to tie round his hand, Mrs Pepperpot thought how odd it was that it was Mr Pepperpot who had tears in his eyes; it was Mr Pepperpot that had broken something, and had hurt himself so that he had to have a bandage on. Very odd indeed!

But if you think this cured Mrs Pepperpot of reading her fortune in a coffee cup you are very much mistaken. The only thing is, she *does* take more care not to pick up the wrong cup and read her husband's fortune instead of her own.

# The Fairy-Tale Boy

Once upon a time there was a little boy who said to his mother, 'I want to go out into the world and kill a dragon, and then I'll bring you back all the gold.'

His mother answered: 'But what about the princess? Won't you set her free as well, pet?'

'I suppose so,' said George, for that was his name, 'as long as I don't have to marry her; 'cos you know I don't like girls.'

'Very well, dear; good luck!' said his mother.

'Oh, but you mustn't say "good luck!" You have to give me food and drink for the journey. I'm going to sit down by the side of the road and start eating, and then an old woman will come or a dwarf, or something like that, and they'll be hungry, and I'll give them all my food, 'cos then they'll help me, you know, to find the way to the dragon and all that.'

'All right, pet, you shall have some food for the journey,' said his mother, and she put three sandwiches in a tin and put them in a little knapsack with a bottle of milk.

So George went out into the world to kill the dragon. And when he had walked a little he came to a road crossing and there he sat down and opened his knapsack and took out a sandwich.

'I 'spect an old woman will come along in a minute, and she'll ask me for food. Then afterwards she's sure to show me the way to the dragon,' he said to himself.

No sooner had he thought this than an old woman *did* come round the corner, walking slowly towards him. When she reached the place where he was sitting she stopped and fixed her eyes on George's sandwich.

'Good afternoon,' said George, and held out his hand with the sandwich in it.

'Good afternoon, my boy,' said the woman; 'you shouldn't play with your food like that.'

'I'm *not* playing with my food,' said George indignantly. 'I'm giving it to you. Aren't you hungry?'

'Of course not,' said the woman. 'I have my lunch before I go out, and so should you, young fellow, and not drag it about with you, leaving dirty bits of paper behind and egg-shells and

I don't know what. Ugh!' And with that she walked off and left George holding his sandwich.

George sat staring after her for a bit.

'Oh well,' he said, 'I suppose there'll be others coming along. She wasn't the right kind of fairy-tale woman, anyway. I'd better eat this sandwich myself while I'm waiting.'

While he was munching the bread he heard a scuffling noise behind the hedge. It was a squirrel.

'Hullo, squirrel! Would you like something to eat?' said George, and threw the second sandwich into the hedge. But the squirrel took fright and bounded away towards a wood.

'Perhaps it wants me to follow it,' thought George. So he picked up his knapsack and walked after the squirrel into the wood. The squirrel, meanwhile, stayed quite still, as if it were really waiting for him, and George was now quite certain that it was going to show him the way to the dragon. When he got quite close the squirrel started leaping from branch to branch and George began to run, stumbling over sticks and stumps, further and further into the wood, until at last they came to a little stream. Here the squirrel jumped lightly from a tree on one side of the stream to another tree on the other side. But George stopped; the stream was too deep for him to wade across, and he was afraid he might drown. So he very sensibly stayed where he was.

Instead he sat down by the edge of the stream and took out his last sandwich. Just then he saw a fish swimming by.

'P'raps you're the one who is going to help me,' he said, and threw the last sandwich into the water. But the fish dodged under a stone and the sandwich floated away down the stream.

George jumped up and followed the bobbing sandwich to see where it would go. Soon the stream widened and ran into a pool, and there on the bank stood a big boy watching a fishing-line.

'Don't make too much noise!' said the big boy. 'You'll frighten the fish away!'

'Sorry!' said George. 'Would you like some milk?' he asked.

'Milk? Are you off your head? How d'you expect me to drink milk while I'm fishing? You scram out of here and be quick about it!'

Well, there was nothing for it; George had to make himself scarce, but he was beginning to feel a little sad. His adventure wasn't turning out quite as he had planned. He sat down in a patch of bilberries and drank up his bottle of milk himself. Then he lay down and took a little nap.

When he woke up there was a little girl standing there, watching him.

'Hullo!' said George.

'Hullo!' said the little girl. 'You looked so

nice, lying there asleep; just like my cousin!
What a smart sandwich tin you've got; I haven't
got one like that with Donald Duck on it.'

'Got it for my birthday,' said George. He was
suddenly feeling very hungry, but there was
nothing left to eat.

'Are you hungry?' asked the little girl. 'I can
give you some food, if you like. I'm bilberrying,
you see, so I've brought a picnic lunch – look!
Sausages and strawberry jelly; it's jolly good!'

'Thank you very much,' said George, and he
ate up two sausages and all the jelly that was left.

The little girl stood watching him, and when
he had finished she said, 'Now you will have to
save me from the dragon.'

'Dragon?' George gulped and the last bit of
jelly went down the wrong way.

'Of course,' she said. 'When you've eaten the princess's food you must kill the dragon. It is lying just down there in the bushes.'

'All right, I'm ready!' said George in his most manly voice. He was a *little* afraid when he started walking over to the bushes. But he picked up a good stout stick – sorry, I mean sword – and smacked the dragon right on the nose. Wham! Afterwards he hacked it into several pieces and then he jumped on them to make quite sure it was dead.

'It's quite safe now, Princess!' he said to the little girl. 'You can come out now!'

'Oh, thank you, St George!' she said. 'Now you can marry me if you like – unless I marry my cousin, of course.'

'You marry your cousin,' said George. 'I don't mind.'

'All right. But you can come home with me if you like, and have some more jelly.'

'No thanks, Princess,' said George. 'You see, I have to look for the gold now that I've killed the dragon.'

And do you know? Under the tree-stump – sorry, I mean the dragon – George found a heap of beautiful pebbles that shone in the sun

like silver when he ran them through his hands. George put them all in his knapsack and was very pleased with his treasure even though it wasn't gold.

After all, you can't expect to find gold under the first dragon that you kill.

# The Ski-Race

Mrs Pepperpot has done a lot of things in her life, and most of them I've told you about already. But now I must tell you how she went ski-racing one day last winter.

Mr Pepperpot had decided to go in for the annual local ski-race. He had been a pretty good skier when he was young, so he said to Mrs Pepperpot:

'I don't see why I shouldn't have a go this year; I feel more fit than I have for many years.'

'That's right, husband, you do that,' said Mrs Pepperpot, 'and if you win the cup you'll get your favourite ginger cake when you come home.'

So Mr Pepperpot put his name down, and when the day came he put on his white anorak and blue cap with a bobble on the top and strings under his chin. He slung his skis over his shoulders and said he would wax them when he got to the starting point.

'Righto! Best of luck!' said Mrs Pepperpot. She was already greasing the cake-tin and stoking the stove for her baking.

'Thanks, wife,' said Mr Pepperpot and went off. It was not before he had turned the corner by the main road that Mrs Pepperpot caught sight of his tin of wax which he had left on the sideboard.

'What a dunderhead that man is!' exclaimed Mrs Pepperpot. 'Now I shall have to go after him, I suppose; otherwise his precious skis are more likely to go backwards than forwards and there'll be no cup in this house today.'

So Mrs Pepperpot flung her shawl round her shoulders and trotted up the road as fast as she could with the tin of wax. When she got near the starting point there was a great crowd gathered. She dodged in and out to try and find her husband, but everyone seemed to be wearing white anoraks and blue caps. At last she saw a pair of sticks stuck in the snow with a blue cap hanging from the top. She could see the initials P.P. sewn in red thread inside.

'That must be his cap,' thought Mrs Pepperpot. 'Those are his initials, Peter Pepperpot. I sewed them on myself in red thread like that. I'll just drop the wax in the cap; then he'll find it when he comes to pick up his sticks.'

As she bent forward to put the wax in the cap she accidently knocked it off the stick and at that moment she shrank so quickly that it was she who fell into the cap, while the tin of wax rolled out into the snow!

'No harm done,' thought Mrs Pepperpot; 'when he comes along he'll see me in his cap. Then he can put me down somewhere out of the way of the race. And as soon as I grow large again I can go home.'

But a moment later a big hand reached down, snatched up the cap and crammed it over a mop of thick hair. The strings were firmly tied and Mrs Pepperpot was trapped!

'Oh well!' she thought. 'I'd better not say anything before the race starts.' For she knew Mr Pepperpot hated to think anybody might get to know about her shrinking.

'Number 46!' she heard the starter shout, 'on your mark, get set, go!' And Number 46, with Mrs Pepperpot in his cap, glided off to a smooth start.

'Somebody must have lent him some wax,' she thought; 'there's nothing wrong with his skis,

anyway.' Then from under the cap she shouted, 'Don't overdo it, now, or you'll have no breath left for the spurt at the end!'

She could feel the skier slow up a little. 'I suppose you know who's under your cap?' she added. 'You had forgotten the wax, so I brought it along. Only I fell into your cap instead of the wax.'

Mrs Pepperpot now felt the skier's head turn round to see if anyone was talking to him from behind.

'It's me, you fool!' said Mrs Pepperpot. 'I've shrunk again. You'll have to put me off by the lane to our house – you pass right by, remember?'

But the skier had stopped completely now.

'Come on, man, get a move on!' shouted Mrs Pepperpot. 'They'll all be passing you!'

'Is it . . . is it true that you're the little old woman who shrinks to the size of a pepperpot?'

'Of course – you know that!' laughed Mrs Pepperpot.

'Am *I* married to *you*? Is it *my* wife who shrinks?'

'Yes, yes, but hurry now!'

'No,' said the skier, 'if that's how it is I'm not going on with the race at all.'

'Rubbish!' shouted Mrs Pepperpot. 'You *must*

go on! I put a cake in the oven before I went out and if it's scorched it'll be all your fault.'

But the skier didn't budge.

'Maybe you'd like me to pop out of your cap and show myself to everybody? Any minute now I might go back to my full size and then the cap will burst and the whole crowd will see who is married to the shrinking woman. Come on, now! With any luck you may just do it, but there's no time to lose; HURRY!'

This worked; the skier shot off at full speed, helping himself to huge strides with his stick. 'Fore!' he shouted as he sped past other skiers.

But when they came to the refreshment stall Mrs Pepperpot could smell the lovely hot soup, and she thought her husband deserved a break. 'We're well up now,' she called. 'You could take a rest.'

The skier slowed down to a stop and Mrs Pepperpot could hear there were many people standing round him. 'Well done!' they said. 'You're very well placed. But what are you looking so worried about? Surely you're not frightened of the last lap, are you?'

'No, no, nothing like that!' said the skier. 'It's this cap of mine – I'm dead scared of my cap!'

But the people patted him on the back and told him not to worry, he had a good chance of winning.

Under the cap Mrs Pepperpot was getting restless again. 'That's enough of that!' she called. 'We'll have to get on now!'

The people who stood nearest heard the voice and wondered who spoke. The woman who ladled out the soup said, 'Probably some loud-speaker.'

And Mrs Pepperpot couldn't help laughing. 'Nearer the truth than you think!' she thought. Then she called out again, 'Come on, husband, put that spurt on, and let's see if we can make it!'

And the skis shot away again, leaping many yards each time the sticks struck into the snow. Very soon Mrs Pepperpot could hear the sound of clapping and cheering.

'What do we do now?' whispered the skier in a miserable voice. 'Can you last another minute? Then I can throw the cap off under the fir trees just before we reach the finishing line.'

'Yes, that will be all right,' said Mrs Pepperpot. And, as the skis sped down the last slope, the strings were untied and the cap flew through the air, landing safely under the fir trees.

When Mrs Pepperpot had rolled over and over many times she found herself growing

big once more. So she got up, shook the snow off her skirt and walked quietly home to her house. From the cheering in the distance she was sure her husband had won the cup.

The cake was only a little bit burnt on the top when she took it out of the oven, so she cut off the black part and gave it to the cat. Then she whipped some cream to put on top and made a steaming pot of coffee to have ready for her champion husband.

Sure enough, Mr Pepperpot soon came home – *without* the cup. 'I forgot to take the wax,' he said, 'so I didn't think it was worth going in for the race. But I watched it, and you should have seen Paul Petersen today; I've never seen him run like that in all my born days. All the same, he looked very queer, as if he'd seen a ghost or something. When it was over he kept talking about his wife and his cap, and he wasn't satisfied till he'd telephoned his house and made sure his wife had been there all the time, watching the race on television.'

Then Mrs Pepperpot began to laugh. And ever since, when she's feeling sad or things are not going just right, all she has to do is to remember the day she went ski-racing in the wrong cap, and then she laughs and laughs and laughs.

Mrs Pepperpot never knows when she's going to shrink
to the size of a kitchen pepperpot, and its usually at the
most inconvenient moments! But being small can be
a lot of fun too – Mrs Pepperpot will meet the little
people in the Magic Wood, be taught to swim by a frog,
and even sit on a mouse's back! A compilation of nine
short stories including: *Mrs Pepperpot in the Magic Wood*
and *Mrs Pepperpot and the Puppet Show.*

978 1 849 41803 4

A day out in the countryside is never an ordinary outing if Mrs Pepperpot's involved. First, she has to be rescued from a mountain of ice cream by a kitten. Then she has to use her wits to outsmart a crafty fox! A compilation of four fantastic short stories including *Mrs Pepperpot's Outing, Mrs Pepperpot Has a Visitor From America, Gapy Gob Gets a Letter From the King* and *Mrs Pepperpot and the Budgerigar.*

978 0 099 57410 1

Little Miss Pepperpot is kept busy all year round, what will she get up to this time? She might very well find herself riding on a cat, being adopted by a hen, saving her friend the moose and cheering up a young girl in hospital. A compilation of twelve stories, one for each month of the year, including *The New Year's Eve Adventure* and *Mrs Pepperpot's Christmas*.

978 0 099 26727 0

Mrs Pepperpot has a little problem – an enormous little problem – she shrinks! And when she does, she finds herself facing all sorts of funny situations of giant-sized proportions! But whether it's a big brown bear or a moose on the loose, clever little Mrs Pepperpot is always ready with some very big ideas. A collection of thirteen short stories including *Mrs Pepperpot Minds the Baby* and *Mrs Pepperpot and the Moose*.

978 0 099 31800 2

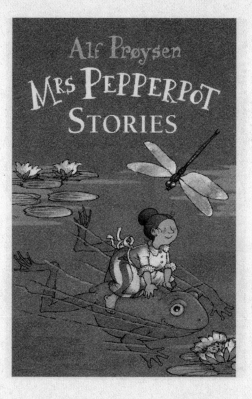

Mrs Pepperpot can't choose when she will shrink to the size of a pepperpot – it just happens! But whatever she encounters, whether it be a monstrous mousetrap, a crafty fox or a gigantic mountain of ice cream, little Mrs Pepperpot will always come out on top. A compilation of forty one classic stories including *Mrs Pepperpot and the Baby Crow* and *Mrs Pepperpot Learns to Swim*.

978 0 099 41139 0

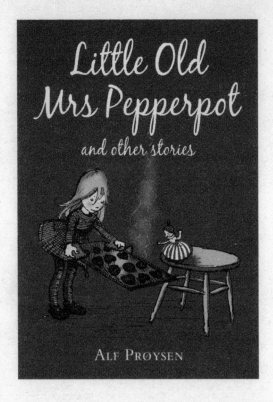

Little Old
Mrs Pepperpot

and other stories

ALF PRØYSEN

Whoever heard of an old woman becoming queen of
the crows? Or riding through the snow on the back of
a cat? Or tricking a mouse into cleaning her house? A
beautiful hardback classic containing twelve entertaining
short stories including *Mrs Pepperpot and the Mechanical
Doll* and *The Potato with Big Ideas.*

978 0 857 54005 8